You're a Gemini

By

Lynne North

Illustrations by

Sanghamitra Dasgupta

Published by

Crimson Cloak Publishing

ISBN 13: 978-1-68160-933-1

ISBN 10: 1-68160-933-9

This book is a work of Fiction. Names, characters, events, or locations are fictitious or used fictitiously. Any resemblances to actual persons or events, living or dead, are entirely coincidental. This book is licensed for private, individual entertainment only. The book contained herein constitutes a copyrighted work and may not be reproduced, stored in or introduced into an information retrieval system or transmitted in any form by ANY means (electrical, mechanical, photographic, audio recording or otherwise) for any reason (excepting the uses permitted by the licensee by copyright law under terms of fair use) without the specific written permission of the author.

©Lynne North 2018

Libraries information

Lynne North

You're A Gemini

1.Juvenile Fiction 2. Illustrated 3. Color 4. Twins 5. Zodiac

Did you know that depending when you were born you have your own zodiac sign? There are twelve signs, and whichever sign you are born under will help determine the type of person you will be. It's all very interesting and funny too! Would you like to know what you are like according to your zodiac sign?

If you are reading this book, then it is probably because your sign is Gemini, but you can work out what sign your friends are too by using the dates on the next two pages!

 Aries are born between March 21st and April 19th

 Taurus are born between April 20th and May 20th

 Gemini are born between May 21st and June 20th

 Cancer are born between June 21st and July 22nd

 Leo are born between July 23rd and August 22nd

 Virgo are born between August 23rd and September 22nd

Libra are born between September 23rd and October 22nd

Scorpio are born between October 23rd and November 21st

Sagittarius are born between November 22nd and December 21st

Capricorn are born between December 22nd and January 19th

Aquarius are born between January 20th and February 18th

Pisces are born between February 19th and March 20th

But of course you want to know about YOU, don't you, because that is most important.

As a Gemini, your symbol is the Twins. You might not have a twin of course, but you will be active enough for two. You are a will-o'-the-wisp, now you see me, now you don't! You will always be on the go doing something. Your energy is amazing. Geminis are known as the social butterflies of the zodiac with good reason.

You are a popular child with a wide group of friends. Your fun, amusing, talkative personality will make you great company, and your friends can consist of many different types of children because you are such a varied character yourself. You get on great with your age group and will always be well liked.

You love to have lots of friends to spend your time with. You are never happier than when you are talking to them, especially if they appear fascinated by what you are saying. You might take your stories a bit too far at times because of the wonderful attention it brings you! You are prone to exaggerate when you see your friends' eyes open even wider about what you are telling them. Don't let your imagination run away with you too much!

You are such a fast mover and quick learner yourself, take care that you don't get impatient of friends who are not quite so bright. They will be interesting and fun in their own ways, and you might hurt their feelings if they think they can't keep up with you.

As a child you are seldom still, and as you grow older that won't change very much. Gemini people are the Peter Pan's of the zodiac, always seeming young and full of life. You are curious with a quick and agile mind, taking in information all the time and loving to pass it on. You are clever and fascinated to know more and more facts.

The world around you is a place to explore and learn, and you are happiest when you are doing both. You flit about like a butterfly from flower to flower, picking up information all the time. In this way, you will know lots of things about many subjects, but might not take the time to learn deeply about any.

Describing your personality can be as difficult as it is to fully understand you. As a Gemini, you are like several children rolled into one. Depending on who you are talking to or mixing with, you can come across as someone completely different. You can also be easily influenced by your friends so try not to let them encourage you to behave badly!

Depending on your mood or the company you are in, you often struggle to make decisions.
Try not to be swayed by the opinions of others.

Your great sense of humour and quick mind will always add to your popularity, as long as you don't expect too much of others.

One thing that makes you stand out as a Gemini child is the variety of your interests. There are so many things you find fascinating, and you are constantly on the look-out for more. This isn't a sign that you are fickle (though you can be!) but that you feel the need to spread yourself wide to make the most of all the wonders and interesting people around you.

You learn early in life that words can give you great power, and you speak better at a younger age than most children. You also struggle to spend time 'learning' anything. You want action and tend to do whatever it is without wasting time learning first.

It is in your nature to give your love and attention to a lot of people rather than one or two. Some friends might feel neglected at times.

As a Gemini you have more interest in working your mind than your body, but that doesn't mean you won't have any interest in sports and hobbies. It might be the opposite. Because you bore so easily, you could change what activities you are interested in on a daily basis!

You will enjoy computer games and puzzles that tax your ever-active mind, but you could also enjoy sports that involve skill. Team sports don't have much appeal, but if you can show how good you are at individual sports in the athletics range, or even tennis, they could hold your interest for a while. You might also enjoy dancing, at least until your mood changes. See how difficult it is to predict what will be going on in a Gemini child's life from day to day?

You love to mix with others. In fact, it is your favourite thing to do. You soak up all the conversations going on around you like a human sponge! Whether you are in your home, school, at a party, at the shops or even in the street, you are always listening, and usually talking too.

Your curiosity is endless. You want to know what everything is, what it does and how it works. You will have been like this since you were a baby and are unlikely to ever change. What might change are specific interests. The most fascinating thing in the world today might be something entirely different tomorrow. Your curiosity is forever; the subject of your interest will change constantly. You are very hard to keep up with!

Your happy, chatty, friendly self does sometimes feel a little sad. The reason might not be obvious to anyone else but you. You mask this new feeling from those around you. You know it will soon change and your happy personality will be back again.

You feel worried that others only love you because you are fun, making them laugh and telling great stories. This isn't true. You don't need to try to control how others feel about you. They love you for who you are, no matter which face you are showing to the world!

When you grow up, you might enjoy a career in teaching, journalism or even politics. Whatever you choose, it will be something that involves lots of communication!

I think you and all your friends will have realised by now that you are very talkative and changeable. These are the two things that stand out most about Gemini. You are the child who should have been born with a telephone in each hand. Need I say more? You can't be happy unless you are communicating in one way or another.

No one will ever know you well because the you they see today is likely to be a different you tomorrow. You are so changeable you probably confuse yourself. As the Twins of the zodiac you live your life as at least two people, quite often as more. It's amazing that you never burn yourself out. Your need to express yourself is the most important thing in your life.

Of all the zodiac signs, you could well be the one that most enjoys change and moving on. Every day is new, with more challenges for you and different things to learn, even another version of you to try out! You love it.

You bore very easily, so you are always on the lookout for fresh things to see and do, different friends to make, more people to talk to. Your life is a blur of finding novel experiences.

But can every day be different like this in the real world?

It can for Gemini. If new things are not happening, you will make them happen! Your amazing mind will not allow a day that doesn't bring up-to-the-minute challenges your way.

There is one last thing to learn about Gemini, your zodiac sign. This is one of the many things you will enjoy discovering. Each zodiac sign has its own ruling planet, and as a Gemini, yours is Mercury.

Being ruled by Mercury is probably the most obvious reason you talk so much, because Mercury is all about communication! You find it easy to talk to anyone. The words flow from you almost without having to think about them and you make the other person feel important.

You are keen to learn about them and the things they know. This is one of the ways you discover so much. You find the world an amazing place and want to know everything about it and the people in it. Mercury helps to guide you in your ceaseless search for information.

So, there you have it. Do you recognise yourself in the pages of this book? If you do, then you are truly a Gemini.

In summary, you are unlikely to ever stop talking. You might even talk in your sleep! You have a quick and clever mind, and a sharp wit. You are fun and exciting to be with, but even you sometimes get a bit upset about something or other. These moods soon pass because you are too lively and cheerful to feel sad for long. Life is for living and is so full of exciting things to see, do and learn. You want to know about every one of them. You probably will soon!

I have enjoyed our little chat. I hope you have too.

Gemini
May 21 - June 20

+ Positive Traits
Adaptable
Outgoing
Intelligent

− Negative Traits
Indecisive
Impulsive
Nosy

Ruling Planet
Mercury

Symbol
"The Twins"

Mode
Mutable

House Ruled
Third

Element
Air

Keyword
Communication

For more coloring and activities, please go to
www.crimsoncloakpublishing.com

About the Author

Lynne North lives in a countryside area in the North West of England. She has a lifetime love of books and reading, and always longed to have a book published. Her first children's fantasy, *"Caution: Witch in Progress"* was launched at Earls Court Book Fair in 2013.

Lynne is now delighted to be an author and Marketing Director for Crimson Cloak Publishing. Her novel 'Be Careful What You Wish For' was released on St. Patrick's Day 2016. *'Caution: Witch in Progress'* was re-released, and *'Zac's Destiny'* also released later in 2016. Lynne has since written a short children's fantasy, two role play game books, and a book of macabre short stories, *'Unlucky For Some'* definitely not for children!

Lynne has taken early retirement from a full time job as a data analyst to dedicate herself to her first love, writing.

https://www.facebook.com/Lynne.North.Author/   http://www.lynnenorth.co.uk/

About the Illustrator

Sanghamitra Dasgupta

Graphic designer, Illustrator, character designer. Sanghamitra is a comic artist with 26 years of cartoon sketching experience. She is innovative and highly creative, good at thinking outside the box when it comes to solving a problem.

https://www.facebook.com/CreativeArtShoppe/

https://www.behance.net/creativeartshoppee

http://worknhire.com/Contractor/Profile/tora1986

https://www.instagram.com/creative_art_shoppee__/

Made in the USA
Las Vegas, NV
17 March 2021